GRANDPA'S
Quilt

By
BETSY FRANCO

Illustrated by
LINDA A. BILD

Children's Press®
A Division of Grolier Publishing
New York London Hong Kong Sydney
Danbury, Connecticut

Grandpa lived with
Anna, Ben, and Lily.

3

Grandpa sat in his bed all winter long.
He read stories to Anna, Ben, and Lily.

Grandpa loved his cozy quilt.
Red and yellow were his favorite colors.

8

But Grandpa's quilt was too short.
His toes were very cold.

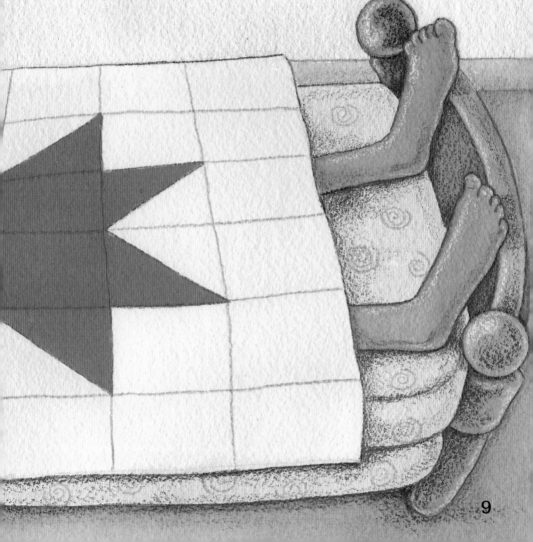

The children turned the quilt around.

Grandpa's toes were still cold!

Anna cut off the top of the quilt.

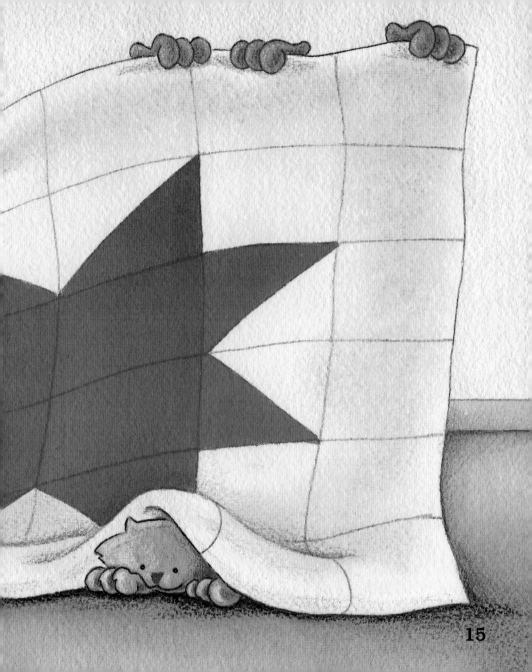

15

She sewed it to the bottom.

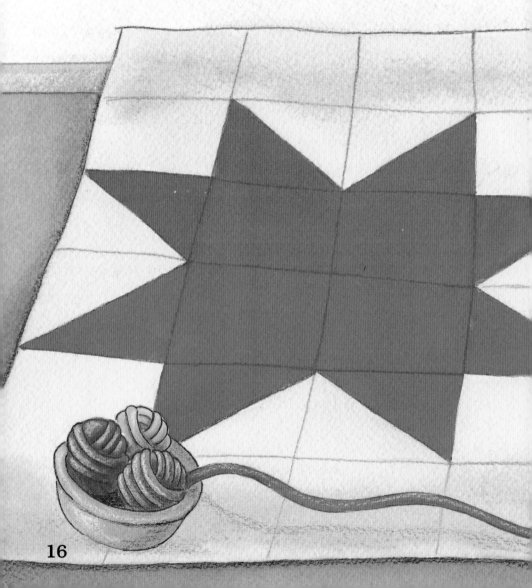

17

18

Grandpa's toes were still cold!

20

Ben cut and sewed.

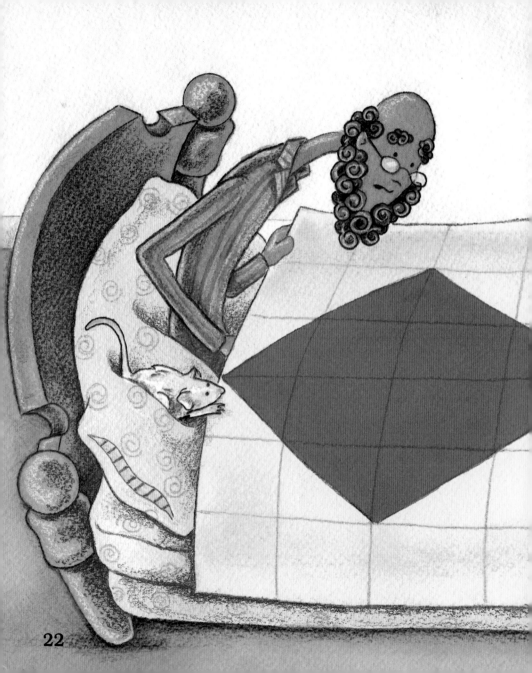

22

He made the red star into a red diamond.

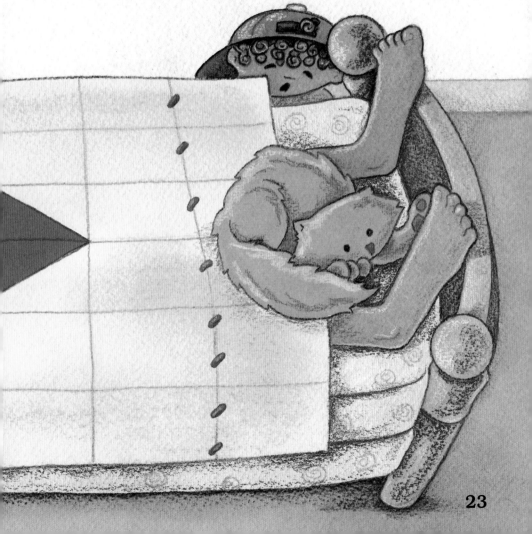

Grandpa's toes were still cold!

Lily cut out all the squares.
She sewed them together again.

27

28

Now, the quilt was long and thin . . .
just like Grandpa!

Grandpa's toes were warm
all winter long!

29

Word List (62 words)

a	cold	into	off	still	very
again	colors	it	out	stories	warm
all	cozy	just	quilt	the	was
and	cut	like	read	them	were
Anna	diamond	Lily	red	thin	winter
around	favorite	lived	sat	to	with
bed	Grandpa	long	sewed	toes	yellow
Ben	Grandpa's	loved	she	together	
bottom	he	made	short	too	
but	his	now	squares	top	
children	in	of	star	turned	

About the Author

Betsy Franco is the author of more than forty books for children—picture books, poetry, and nonfiction. She is the only female in her home in Palo Alto, California, where she lives with her husband, three sons, and her cat, Lincoln. Betsy likes to write in the wee hours of the morning when everyone but Lincoln is asleep.

About the Illustrator

Linda Bild grew up in Nebraska and received a B.F.A. in art from Columbia College. Her illustration and design career has taken her to faraway places to live, such as Hong Kong, London, and Montreal. She has illustrated numerous books and materials for children and has directed and illustrated over a dozen educational children's CD-ROMS, receiving several awards. She currently splits her residency between California and Iowa.